Sandra L. Fielden is an occupational psychologist. After working in the Manchester Business School for 20 years, she is now an honorary senior lecturer at the University of Manchester. She has authored five academic books, edited six more, and has written numerous academic papers. Sandra has owned cats for the last 40 years. She also volunteers as a recruitment and induction officer at the local Cats Protection Branch. Most of the cats featured in the book are, or have been, owned by Sandra and her husband, Stuart. The others have been owned by friends.

Lynn D. Radcliffe has been working in product development with high-class retailers for the past 20 years, and has worked with children in developing their creative skills. She has been a volunteer with the Women's Institute for the last 31 years, and with the Royal Volunteers Service for the past 20 years, specifically with library services.

What is the Magic Word?

THE MAGICAL POWER OF PLEASE AND THANK YOU

Written by Sandra L. Fielden and Lynn D. Radcliffe

AUSTIN MACAULEY PUBLISHERS™

LONDON · CAMBRIDGE · NEW YORK · SHARJAH

A CIP catalogue record for this title is available from the British Library.

ISBN 9781398424111 (Paperback)
ISBN 9781398424128 (ePub e-book)

www.austinmacauley.com

First Published 2022
Austin Macauley Publishers Ltd®
1 Canada Square
Canary Wharf
London
E14 5AA

To all children and kitty cats everywhere

Penny is five-year-old cat, who dreams of becoming a ninja warrior, and these are the adventures of Penny and her friends. This first book follows her as she tries to find the magic word that will allow her to have a ninja warrior birthday party.

She was all in black, as she crept along the wall with her minion, Jacob, who was dressed in different shades of brown.

She whispered quietly, "Are you ready? This time we have to take her down. Such evil cannot be allowed to carry on in our homeland."

He nodded and adjusted his dark brown mask which covered his eyes. Penny took a sneak-peak around the end of the wall and there she was, Princess Liberty. Beautiful, as she was clever. A known spy, Liberty wore white furs and diamonds with a black cloak drawn down over her face. Her bodyguard, Alex James the Great, was by her side. He rarely left. Alex James, in his tuxedo, was twice the size of both Penny and Jacob, but Penny was not scared. They had taken him before and they could do it again.

Penny gave Jacob the signal and they both leapt gracefully. Two ninja warriors in the night attacking a cruel, yet beautiful, spy. Alex James saw a movement just to his left and started moving to cover Princess Liberty, but it was too late. Penny was on Liberty, rolling around, fighting, neither holding back. Jacob, too, had found his mark and had knocked the wind out of Alex James, before he, too, threw himself into the fight. Alex James had been too focused on Penny and did not see her brown minion just moments behind her. It was a bad mistake. What seemed like minutes were actually but only moments when Princess Liberty cried for them to stop.

Penny stood tall as she asked them, "So, do you give in to the mighty ninja warrior Penny and my minion Jacob?"

Liberty looked deep into her eyes and said, "You both have to stop this, you know I don't like it, and if you do not stop, I will tell your mum."

Alex James, Penny's older brother, nodded wisely and added, "You know she has warned you before, and if you do it again, I will tell her tonight over tea."

Penny turned away and smiled, she knew he was just threatening to tell on her because she was better than them.

Penny and Jacob walked back home together and, like all of their friends, they lived in a basement flat in an apartment block next to the park. Penny lived with her mum, dad, and brother, Alex James. And from their flat you could see straight to the park where she and her friends played. She did not understand why her friends could not see that she had to practice if she was to be a proper ninja warrior when she grew up. She had taken Jacob under her wing as her minion. As his dad worked away, so it was just his mum and older sister, Liberty, at home. Jacob wasn't sure if he wanted to be a ninja warrior when he grew up but he did like playing in the park. Penny's other friends were Jacob's sister Jessica, Thomas and his brother, Murray. They all had been on the receiving end of Penny's ninja warrior training, even though her mum had warned her to stop. They had also heard all about her ninja warrior birthday party, and that her mum wanted some magic word before she would let Penny have her party.

Penny had been asking her mum if she could have a party for what seemed like forever. Every time she asked, her mum she just said, "Hmm, if you can tell me the magic word, you can have a party."

Penny knew that real ninja warriors used lots of magic, like appearing or disappearing at will. She had been reading about ninja magic but she could not find the magic word her mum was talking about. Penny asked all of her friends what the magic word was: Jacob thought it had to be *abracadabra*, Liberty and Thomas said it must be *alakazam* but Jessica said they were all wrong and it was hocus pocus, as she had seen on TV. Murray was sure it was *bibbidi-bobbidi-boo*, because he had seen it in a film. Penny tried them all out on her mum but every time her mum just said, "That is not the magic word I am looking for, so no party."

She was so worried, she even asked her older brother Alex James, who laughed. He said that she should try *ala peanut butter sandwiches*, which they used on Sesame Street. She knew he was making fun of her but she tried it anyway, her mum stared at her and shook her head.

It was now just three days until her birthday, and Penny was starting to think that she would never work out what the magic word was. She was so upset she did not want to train to be a ninja warrior or play with her friends. She wanted to be alone, so she went for a walk in the park by herself. After she had been walking for what seemed like a really long time, she saw a boy she hadn't seen before. He dressed in different shades of orange and he told her that because of that everyone called him Pepper. He asked her why she looked so upset, so she told him the story of the magic word and her birthday party. Pepper started to laugh and he laughed and he laughed until tears ran down his face. Penny was getting angrier and angrier, she shouted at him that he was mean and she wished she had never met him.

Pepper stopped laughing and said that he did not mean to make her angry, but he could not believe that she was almost five years old and still did not know the magic word her mum wanted her to say.

Penny shouted at him, saying that he was being mean and was making fun of her, that if he knew the word he should just tell her.

He replied that he would only tell her the magic word if she would invite him to her ninja warrior birthday party.

Half-heartedly, Penny said that if her mum let her have a party, because of the magic word he told her, he could come to the party.

Pepper then said that it was very simple; she just had to *say please.*

Penny said that it could not be that simple, as it was a magic word that her mum wanted her to say.

"*How is please a magic word?*" she asked.

He told her that she should go home and ask her mum again about the party and she should say, '*Please, may I have a ninja warrior birthday party.*' He promised it would work, so Penny ran home to try it out on her mum.

Penny told her mum exactly what Pepper had said that she should say, '*Please, may I have a ninja warrior birthday party?*'

Her mum looked shocked and said, "Yes, of course, you can, but how did you find out the magic word?"

Penny told her all about Pepper and that he thought it was funny she did not know that it was the word please that was magic.

Penny was so happy, she ran around to Jacob's house to tell him that she could have a party and that they needed to start planning what games and food she was going to have. After a while Penny wanted to go and tell all of her friends about it, so they went to the park. Penny told them all about Pepper and what he had told her, they could not believe that the magic word was *please*. Jessica said that she could not understand how *please* was a magic word, as everyone knew that magic words were things like *hocus pocus* or *abracadabra*. Penny said she did not know why *please* was a *magic word* but it worked and now she could have a birthday party. She told all of her friends that they had to go and ask if they could come to her ninja warrior birthday party. Making sure that they had to use the magic word, or else they may not be allowed to come. When her friends had all left to go and ask if they could go to the party, she went to find Pepper. She ran over and told him the good news and asked him to explain why *please* was a magic word.

He explained to her that it is polite to say please and that it made grown-ups happy. It showed respect and it was expected by adults. She said that, as he had come up with the magic word, he could come to her party, although he had to wear a ninja mask, as they would be playing lots of ninja warrior games.

On the day of the party, Penny was up before everyone else, as she was excited. She still found it hard to believe that please was the magic word but, as it had worked, she didn't care. She put on her ninja warrior mask and ran to wake up the rest of the family and then she went over to Jacob's apartment to see if he was up and ready. Together, they ran over to the park to start planning out where everything would be going, the table for the food and drinks, and another table for presents. Penny had told all of her friends that she wanted her birthday presents to be about ninja warriors. Later that day, the tables were all laid out and filled with food, drinks and presents. All her friends were there and she introduced her new friend Pepper to everyone.

After lots of games and a ninja warrior birthday cake that Penny's mum had made, Penny opened her birthday presents. She got lots of books about ninja warriors, as well as ninja warrior pyjamas from Jacob, Jessica and Thomas, plus a ninja warrior duvet set from her mum, dad and brother. At the end of opening all of her presents, Penny noticed that there wasn't a present from Pepper. She knew that they had only been friends for a short time, but she thought he might have brought something small. Then she felt bad, because if it was not for Pepper, there would have been no birthday party, so in a way, that was his gift to her.

Yet, as if he knew, Pepper wished her happy birthday and he asked if she had noticed that there wasn't a present from him. She told him that he was the reason she got a birthday party and that was the best present anyone could give her.

He smiled and said that he did have a present for her and there was someone he wanted her to meet. Just then, there was a flash of light and out of the smoke appeared a real-life grand master ninja warrior.

Penny could not believe her eyes and she thought she may burst from happiness. The rest of the children just stared, their mouths open. The grand master ninja warrior told them his name was Blue, and they sat at his feet while he told them lots of stories. After, he told Penny that he had been watching her training, and when she was older, if she continued to train hard, she could become a real ninja warrior. She had so many questions that no one else had a chance to ask Blue anything but, as it was her birthday party, they did not mind too much. At the end, he told her that it would be hard work and she would have to train every day but he promised to help her to become a real ninja warrior. When he was finished, he told her he would be watching over her and then just disappeared in a flash of smoke.

Penny did not think she could ever have a better birthday present and ran up to Pepper to give him a really big hug. She was so excited, she had to keep telling him how she was definitely going to be a real ninja warrior when she grew up. She told him she did not know what to say to him, as there were no words good enough.

He smiled at her and told her that there was another magic word for just this sort of thing.

She looked at him and said that she did not know there was another one.

Pepper laughed until Penny looked so annoyed she might just explode. He told her that she had a lot to learn and that, although you say please when you were asking for something, when you had received something you should say *thank you*.

Penny asked him if thank you had the same magic properties as please, he told her to try it out.

First, she ran to her parents and said, "*Thank you* for my birthday party."

They smiled, hugged her and told her she was welcome.

Then she told all of her friends *thank you* for their presents and that thank you was another magic word they could use.

Finally, she ran back to Pepper, kissed him on the check and said, "*Thank you*."

The End

CPSIA information can be obtained
at www.ICGtesting.com
Printed in the USA
LVHW070528150622
721261LV00016B/412

9 781398 424111